REMARKABLY
ruby

REMARKABLY
ruby

TERRI LIBENSON

BALZER + BRAY
An Imprint of HarperCollins*Publishers*

Balzer + Bray is an imprint of HarperCollins Publishers.

Remarkably Ruby
Copyright © 2022 by Terri Libenson
All rights reserved. Printed in the United States of America.
No part of this book may be used or reproduced in any manner whatsoever without
written permission except in the case of brief quotations embodied in critical articles
and reviews. For information address HarperCollins Children's Books, a division of
HarperCollins Publishers, 195 Broadway, New York, NY 10007.
www.harpercollinschildrens.com

Library of Congress Control Number: 2021950856
ISBN 978-0-06-313919-0 (hardcover) — ISBN 978-0-06-313918-3 (pbk.)

Typography by Terri Libenson and Laura Mock
22 23 24 25 26   PC/WOR   10 9 8 7 6 5 4 3 2 1
❖
First Edition

To my remarkable readers:
I'm always grateful

PROLOGUE:
RUBY

I'm not what you would call a people person.

It's not that I don't try. I do. But most of the time, making friends in middle school is a huge chore. I don't have the greatest social skills.

I also don't have a lot in common with the kids around here. Most of them are into things I'm not, like dances, social media, and sports.

Me?

Back in grade school, it was another story. There were a couple kids I was close to. And yep, they were also a little different, which helped.

But one moved away in fifth grade. And since I didn't get a phone until this year, we didn't really stay in touch.

our pen pal agreement was one-sided

And the other . . . well, we had a falling-out.

I'll get to that later. In the meantime, it's just:

Me, myself, and I

Déjà vu

I'm mostly okay with it. People don't pick on me or anything. They leave me alone.

helps that I'm the same height as some of my teachers

Besides, my mom says that the most important thing is to be "a strong, independent person." So that's what I'm attempting to do. And I think I'm succeeding.

scribble scribble scritch

On the outside, anyway.

RUBY

It all began in fourth grade. That's when I shot up.

And by "shot up," I mean "grew to the size of our money tree."

both have braids
and tall trunks

I love that tree. It's supposed to bring good fortune. (I'm still waiting on that.) My mom keeps it in the corner of the living room* near a window. So that it "thrives."

*If your house is older, you probably have a formal living room—which, in our house, never gets used except at midnight, when our cat gets the "zoomies."

We have a ton of plants in that living room. Our cat, Buford, likes to hide behind them. He probably imagines he's a jungle tiger, ready to pounce.

prey

I'm in charge of watering the plants. That's my main chore and I'm good at it.

healthy, happy plants

I find it kinda funny that when a plant gets nice and big, it's "robust" and "thriving." But when I did . . .

It makes my "aloneness" more noticeable.

Speaking of alone . . . right now, I'm in the restroom at school by myself. It's early, right before homeroom. My stomach is kind of bugging me. That happens sometimes. I've been to the doctor. She calls it a "nervous stomach," which is a nice way of saying what I really have:

IBS:
Irritable
Bowel
Syndrome

↑

or as I call it, "Irritating
Bathroom Struggles"

I've heard some kids call me "Baked Bean Girl," which is another way of putting it. It's 'cause I once had to rush to the restroom after a lunch of . . . Well, you get the idea. I told my mom, who thought it was funny and wanted to make me a T-shirt:

I didn't think it was that funny.

Anyway, I deal with it. I've stopped announcing my latest meals, anyway. And stopped eating stuff on the doctor's "do not ingest" list, like:

I leave the stall and try to find an open sink. It's not easy. This is the busiest restroom time, other than after lunch. It really bugs me that girls come in and hog the sinks to put on makeup and brush their hair and stuff, when there are people who actually need to wash up. It's not like they can't get ready at their lockers.

full-length mirrors

vanity lights

pencil/lipgloss holder

I don't know what to say to that. Sarah Reyes is really nice—one of the nicer kids in my grade—but it's not like I know anything about making clothes.

I finally think of something to say.

Hearts are tool.

She looks confused, smiles awkwardly, and leaves.

I meant to say, "Hearts are totally cool." Ughh!

I finally find a sink. A girl makes room, looking a little scared of me.

Being bigger than most kids sometimes has that effect on people, mainly sixth graders who don't know me. Doesn't help that I've accidentally knocked a few of them down.

I leave the restroom and head to homeroom. Mrs. Winn, my favorite teacher (English), is walking in my direction.

That's the school's art and literary magazine. Mrs. Winn always asks me and a bunch of other kids to submit.

A few months ago, Mrs. Winn encouraged me to enter my poem (an English assignment) in the Student Showcase. That's a big event around here. Kids show off their history and science projects, stories, and artwork. There's a contest for each category.

An' guess what?

Yep! I won the poetry contest. I was totally shocked. I didn't even want to enter in the first place.

The thing is, I don't like attention. It just makes . . . well, me . . . that much more obvious to everyone.

But now I'm glad she entered it. 'Cause it made me want to write even more.

my journal ←

almost filled up

I write all the time now. I mean, I always wrote in my journal and stuff, but then I started turning some of those journal entries into actual things.

short stories

poetry

badly illustrated poetry

Usually they're about feelings, but sometimes they're also about little things I notice. Things a lot of people don't pay attention to. (When you're alone a lot, that's what happens.)

Like shoelaces.

You can tell a lot about a person by how they tie their shoes.

I once wrote an entire poem comparing people to shoelaces using what Mrs. Winn calls:

As for the Showcase poem—I wrote that about making patterns with my fingers on my fogged-up kitchen window in the morning. I really do that. It kind of calms me.

And as my nervous stomach knows, I could use some calming.

She leaves and I head for homeroom.

I feel my stomach act up again, but I ignore it.

I walk into homeroom and sit at my usual desk in the second-to-last row. Lindsay Donsky and Kyle Duncan sit in front of me and secretly text each other (as usual). Quiet Girl (Emmie Douglass) sketches away in her notebook. She quickly holds it up to show her best friend, Brianna, who sits across the room. I can't see the drawing, but Brianna giggles and gives her a thumbs-up.

Sometimes I pretend I'm like them.

But this time I don't. Instead, I take out my social studies note-book so I can finish an assignment, and I tell myself the same thing that I do every morning at this time:

WE JUST GOT THE GO-AHEAD TO PUT UP POSTERS AFTER SCHOOL FOR THE ELECTION, WHICH IS IN (gulp) A MONTH.

WE'RE NOT ALLOWED TO GIVE AWAY REAL CANDY, SO WE DREW THEM INSTEAD.

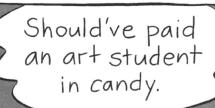

Should've paid an art student in candy.

LIKE ME, JOSH BENTZ IS RUNNING FOR NEXT YEAR'S CLASS PRESIDENT. UNLIKE ME:

He doesn't seem to be taking it too seriously.

Which makes me both happy and furious.

27

IT'S BEEN HAPPENING MORE
AND MORE. THE THING I
ALWAYS THINK ABOUT BUT
NEVER TALK ABOUT:

three's becoming
a crowd

WE HEAD IN OPPOSITE
DIRECTIONS.

Later, Meema!

← my
silly Three
Musketeers*
name

* also a
candy

30

31

WE MET IN SEVENTH GRADE P.E. WHEN HE ACCIDENTALLY BONKED ME ON THE FOREHEAD WITH A FLAGPOLE.

WE KINDA FLIRTED FOR AN ENTIRE YEAR. BUT WE WERE STILL A LITTLE SHY WITH EACH OTHER.

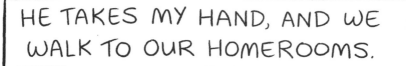

HE TAKES MY HAND, AND WE WALK TO OUR HOMEROOMS.

love that everyone sees us together

hoping to make "cutest couple" in yearbook

THE FIRST TIME TREVOR KISSED ME WAS A WEEK AGO.

BUT WE CAN BE AWKWARD TOGETHER AND IT DOESN'T MATTER.

didn't know where to put lips ← left? right? braces stuck together!

(also, we've improved) Try again?

37

RUBY

I'm in Mrs. Winn's second-period English class. My favorite.

Well, except for one thing.

I can't wait until we change seats.

↑
every quarter

hoping to be
farther from
people and
closer to
pencil sharpener

Okay, class.
Let's start.

Yesterday, we
discussed imagery.

For homework, I had you
write a two-stanza poem
using figurative language...
or to put it more — *ahem* —
poetically...

...to paint a picture
with words.

To get the ball rolling, I'd like to read an excerpt that uses imagery and stirs the senses.

"The night was creeping on the ground;
She crept and did not make a sound
Until she reached the tree, and then
She covered it, and sole again

Along the grass beside the wall.
I heard the rustle of her shawl
As she threw blackness everywhere
Upon the sky and ground and air."

She clears her throat.

41

*crickets
chirping*

Oh, come on. I know there
are several budding writers
here.

This is a
nonjudgmental
zone, I promise.

Great! Leah.

It's okay, come
on up.

Her eyes scan the room. Could be my imagination, but I feel like they pause on me for more than a couple seconds.

And I don't know why; maybe it's my showcase prize, and the fact that I kinda like what I wrote, but suddenly . . .

⟨deep breath⟩

"Muffled music that
floats through the wall,
into my room,
and into my head
is heavy,
like a weighted blanket.

"The soft rhythm
reminds me of old days
and old times;
it smothers me mightily
with its melody."

I catch Joe and Anthony whispering to each other, but I can't tell if it's about me.

I want to die. Why did I do this??

A few kids raise their hands. Mrs. Winn calls on one.

Thank you, Ruby. Great job.

That cheers me instantly. I still can't believe I volunteered.

Anyone else?

A couple more kids go up. One recites a poem about a snowy night (which makes me cold). Kyle Duncan reads about a cheese-and-mustard sandwich (which makes me hungry). Imagery sure is powerful.

When the bell rings, Mrs. Winn calls me over.

Ruby, there's something I've been thinking about for a while. Something I think you'd be perfect for.

I wait.

I'd like to start an after-school poetry club. We'd pick themes to write about, read, share ideas, that sort of thing.

I got permission from the principal. Would you be interested?

We'd meet twice a week, Monday and Thursday.

Huh. A poetry club.

thinking
face

It's nice that she asked, but truth is, I've never wanted to try after-school stuff. I just don't fit in anywhere.

The two shyest (but most talented) kids in our class. I don't know if I'm as good. Maybe my winning poem was just a freak thing.

But . . .

. . .it could be fun. And more exciting than writing in my room.

I leave and head to third period, thinking, just like I said I'd do.

Maybe I should leave the thinking to later.

Mia

RIGHT. WHICH LETS OUT... NOW.

improv kids
very loud

I'M SO DISTRACTED BY TREVOR, I ALMOST MISS DEV.

Hi.

Keya's brother

Dad's waiting in front.

Okay. See you guys later.

Don't worry, Meema. You've got this.

58

HE HELPS US HANG THE REST OF THE POSTERS.

resisting the urge to lean over and—

VZZZZ VZZZ

My mom. You guys need a ride?

Go 'head. Gabs and I are walking home.

HE WAVES GOODBYE, AND SOON ENOUGH, WE LEAVE, TOO.

You think Josh would really do that?

Well, what if he did? Would you do the same? Like, bribe the girls?

What? No way.

I WOULDN'T EVEN KNOW WHAT TO GIVE THEM. IT'S NOT LIKE I HAVE A POOL.

See? No matter what happens, that's why you'd make the best prez.

You always do the right thing.

RUBY

Back at home, I try to avoid my nosy mom, but she corners me.

My mom is a sculptor. That is, she makes ceramic pots, vases, candlesticks, and her specialty: little figurines. She sells them in local galleries and online. They're pretty nice. But we can't escape them—they're everywhere in our house.

With all her clay creatures, it's like living in the Amazon . . . but with the wrong animal species.

One thing about my mom and me—we look a lot alike.

same build, same hair color, same freckles...

... in the same places! (Little Dipper-shaped constellations across our cheeks)

But that's where it ends. My mom has a lot more energy. And is kinda high-strung. She calls this her "artistic temperament."

I just think she needs an off button.

Maybe—dare I ask—even the ceramics club?

Her voice scales up hopefully.

giggle

Dream on.

My mom worries about me . . . a lot. She thinks I'm antisocial and wants me to "get involved." But the last place I want to involve myself any longer than I have to is at school.

Usually, I'd change the subject and say I've gotta do homework or something, but I finally have an answer that'll make her day. Maybe her year.

Actually...

YES?

I think of a million reasons. I'm worried no one will like what I write. Or I won't think of anything good. Or it'll be boring, it'll be awkward, the other kids will hate me, I'll hate them, and so on and so on and—

But I smile. A little.

I know this sounds mean, but . . . anything to get her off my back.

She blows me a kiss and goes back in her studio.

I stand there for a minute, wondering what I just agreed to.

Yeah, I know in the whole big scheme of things, joining a poetry club is no big deal. It's nothing. But . . .

. . . it's a huge step for me. I haven't joined anything since elementary school. And those weren't exactly wild successes.

frozen →

Ballet class:

THUNK

playing the recorder:

Art class:

I know, I know, this is different. But back then, I thought I'd be good at that stuff, too.

So how can I be sure?

Mia

Not my bedtime for another nine minutes and thirty-two seconds.

Thirty-one.

HE GLANCES AT MY NEW-BUT-OLD-LOOKING RECORD PLAYER.

scrikka

makes scratching sounds

bought with birthday $

You know people were *happy* when music progressed beyond that, right?

You've only told me a million times.

I DON'T SAY ANYTHING. MOSTLY 'CAUSE I DON'T WANNA ARGUE.

SOMETIMES DAD JUST
DOESN'T GET ME.

RUBY

Me and my big mouth.

    I'm in Mrs. Winn's room, right before first period. It's on my way. Thought I'd pop in and tell her the good news.

Wonderful, Ruby! So glad you're joining the club.

And as part of your new membership responsibilities...

...I'd like you to help recruit other students.

What?

I don't... get it. Don't you already have members?

Mrs. Winn gets a funny look on her face.

Well...

Right now it's just you and Leah. Kieran has violin lessons and swim practice, so he's out.

Maybe you and Leah could make posters and hang them up? And ask some friends to join?

uh. Friends?

urrghhel

last night's veggie tostada acting up

Mrs. winn grins in that pleading way that reminds me too much of my mom.

But it's one thing to say no to a parent. It's another to say no to your favorite teacher.

Okay.

sigh

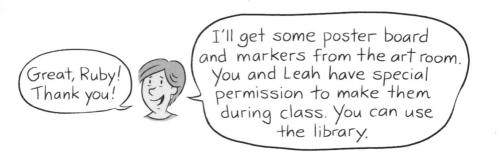

Little Leah who's even quieter than me?

I'm regretting this already.
I head to first period. It's the only time that history class flies.

I return to Mrs. Winn's to collect our supplies. Leah is already there, holding a stack of poster board bigger than she is. Mrs. Winn gives me a set of markers. Leah and I head to the library—which, luckily, is right down the hall. That means we don't have to do anything awful like:

In the library, Ms. Regas points us to a table in back. We sit down silently. But then Leah smiles kinda shyly at me and holds up a notebook.

I thought of something in first period. Maybe it's silly, I dunno....

If **YOU** like verse and eating grub, come join us at our **POETRY CLUB!**
First meeting:
Monday after school, room 216
BYOG (bring your own grub—no nuts)

We sit and think. After a minute or two, I come up with some ideas.

Huh. This isn't so bad.

If you like poems,
rap, and verse,
come join us
Monday
March the first!

Uh. It's, like, a near-rhyme, but...

I love it!

Yeah?

Yeah. Wanna draw 'em out?

We do. We use markers in every color. I even illustrate a poster in my famous block letters (perfected in third grade). Soon, I'm not worrying about small talk and stuff. We bounce more ideas off each other.

Are there any good words that rhyme with flan? I make really good flan and I can bring some to the first meeting.

Is that the dessert that looks like a giant booger?

She gets this stunned look, like I just dumped flan in her lap. Oh no, me and my big mouth. I'm such a—

HA HA
HA HA HA

My brother calls it "booger cake." That's why I'm laughing.

I laugh, too.

Before we know it, we have a stack of finished posters . . . including one with flan (rhymed with "spawn"—don't ask). And no time to spare. The bell's about to ring.

Wanna hang these up at lunch?

uh. Okay.

The bell rings. We take the posters back to Mrs. Winn's and separate for third period.

I head to gym. Not my favorite class.

But for the first time walking there . . .

. . . I'm smiling.

Mia

94

TREVOR IS DOING AN IMPROV ROUTINE. HE'S GOOD, EVEN GETS AUDIENCE MEMBERS TO JOIN HIM.

SO, THERE'S A POETRY CLUB.
AND RUBY'S JOINING.
I GUESS THAT'S GOOD.

'Cause she really needs new friends.

I'M DISTRACTED BY A BUNCH OF BOYS HEADING TO THE CAF. ONE OF THEM IS JOSH.

always smiling
but not in an annoying way...
...which is so annoying

RUBY

Just spotted Mia outside the cafeteria, checking out my poster.

I remember when she was a fellow dork. Seems like a zillion years ago.

Okay, never mind that. It's time to start recruiting members. Glad I'm not doing it alone.

one shy girl $+$ one loner girl $=$ twice the bravery

We made a flyer from one of the posters and photocopied it. Leah's idea, not Mrs. Winn's. I'm already impressed.

← ~~shy~~
resourceful

Second lunch period is crowded with seventh and eighth graders. Kinda intimidating, but that's where we can find more kids at once. My idea this time. Don't know if it's a good or bad idea, but it's someplace to start. We agree to avoid:

jocks and other popular people

chomp
chomp

And hit up:

bookish and artsy types

chew chew

They aren't hard to find since the cafeteria is divided into obvious cliques.

Second Lunch Period (a handy blueprint):*

- ← ice cream freezer
- doors
- cashier (nice or mean, depending on day)
- table
- windows
- bench
- art club & manga kids
- science clubs kids
- orchestra & band kids
- swim team; other cool kids
- volleyball team
- basketball team
- tray shelf thing
- lunch odors (good or bad, depending on day)
- dirty tray conveyer belt
- garbage
- ←(stinky)
- mystery place where trays land
- recycling
- windows

*(shamelessly stolen from TRULY TYLER)

We spot some harmless-looking seventh graders at a table near the back and approach them.

107

They don't hear her.

I plop a stack of flyers in front of them. A little too hard.

After giving me a weird look, they each pick one up.

A skinny kid walks over holding a cafeteria tray. On it are chicken nuggets that are supposed to be shaped like stars but look like bloated frogs.

drizzled ketchup adds a grisly touch

Hi. Ruby, right?

Yeah.

I think my sister, Keya, knows you.

I nod.

You might wanna talk to her. She likes poetry.

I don't say anything.

Helpful.

Leah and I look at each other. We grab the stack and leave. Leah points to a quiet corner, and we head over.

I glance to my right.

I shake my head.

She points to a more "eclectic" (Winn Word of the Week!) table near the windows.

I nod. We head over.

After a moment of hesitation, they all shake their heads. A couple girls give us the up-and-down look, which at first makes me mad and then makes me wanna hide behind the tray conveyor belt.

113

That doesn't come out as nice as I'd hoped.

A girl takes one, and we walk away. Quickly.

We're getting nowhere. And wow, they were snobbier than they looked.

I'm ready to give up. I might just quit myself. I mean, what kind of club has only two members?

other than the short-lived
Goldfish Appreciation Club:

But I remember Mrs. Winn, who really wants to get this going.

I rack my brain, trying to think. I notice a bunch of rowdy kids playing Frisbee with a dirty plate (Joe and his friends, ew). Then I spot someone.

Uh. I've got an idea.

I tell Leah my plan. Her eyes get really big and she nods in agreement. We head out.

Leah and I stop in the hallway. The bell rings.

Meet you after school, then?

I nod.

I know that was a total flop, but I still had fun. If you wanna do homework together sometime and hang out, that'd be fun, too.

Really?

Sure. If...you want.

I don't think Leah has many friends, either. She probably worked up all her nerve to ask me.

The second bell's about to ring. I leave quickly, not wanting to be late for health. Not that Mr. Bauman's mean or anything, but I've already gotten a few tardy slips. And I hate, hate, hate everyone staring at me when I come in late.

She helps me pick up the papers.

Why did I say that?

I nod rapidly.

Really? We might get **three** members?

Sarah waves and leaves.

Just when I started to think this was a total waste of time.

Maybe that was worth the tardy bell.

I HIDE BEHIND A LOCKER WHILE TREVOR RUNS OVER.

Hey, you okay?

Nice toddler pants!

yank

Shut up!

THEY DISPERSE, STILL GIGGLING.

Uh. Thanks. Gotta go.

dust

dust

RUBY

I'm such a dweebert!

↳ word that Mia and I
used back when we
were still talking

I haven't had a stomach attack in ages. But I started thinking
about poetry club and got super nervous. Tomorrow is the first

meeting. I've never been in a club. I don't know what to expect, and I'm one of the recruiters!

And then there's Mia.

She didn't even help me after I fell in front of everyone.

The door opens slowly.

I wipe my eyes again.

Whatever.

I, uh, have to go. Election stuff.

Yeah. I wouldn't want to <u>embarrass</u> you before the big day.

She throws me an awkward look and leaves, closing the door. I wait while my eyes turn from red to pink. Glad I walk home instead of taking the bus. I can stay here till my eyes are dry.

Waiting gives me time to notice stuff:

fake nail clippings — fake eye-lashes — real dead rodent

This isn't the first time I've done something like that in front of Mia. I don't know why it keeps happening. Worst part is, I know she's Miss Perfect and I know we have nothing in common anymore and that she's embarrassed to be around me.

Which is why I'm not just mad at her. I'm also mad at:

Me, myself, and I

We're back!

'Cause if I had a perfect life, with perfect friends and a perfect bf with a good chance of becoming class prez . . .

. . . I wouldn't want a klutzo dork ruining it for me, either.

light pinkish

I open the door, make sure the hall is empty . . .

. . . and pray no one sees me.

Mia

139

I KNOW SHE DOESN'T MEAN TO BE THAT WAY. SHE'S A GOOD PERSON. SHE'S JUST SO...SO...

argh... *Ruby.*

WHICH MEANS I'VE *REALLY* GOTTA KEEP MY DISTANCE. ESPECIALLY DURING THE ELECTION.

VZZZZ_{zz}

Wanna have a sleepover tomorrow? Late start on Wednesday. My parents said it's okay.

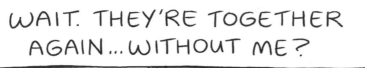

WAIT. THEY'RE TOGETHER AGAIN... WITHOUT ME?

chewed

BLATTT

OH YEAH, BAND RECITAL. MUST'VE JUST ENDED.

happier

I'll ask my parents.

Sounds fun.

142

RUBY

First poetry club meeting.

I'm pretty happy with the turnout. A few days ago, Leah and I went to Mr. Taleb's room. He's the eighth-grade English teacher in charge of the school's book club.

We nodded.

Guess Mr. Taleb came through. There are some kids here we don't recognize.

Also, one of the science kids from the cafeteria.

Go figure.

When we first arrived, Mrs. Winn had us do introductions and share our other interests.

Everyone has a lot of hobbies.

Except me.

All eyes look my way.

I glance down in panic. I can't think of anything I like to do except watch TV, water plants, and . . .

My voice trails off.

When I look up, I'm surprised to see that they all seem kinda interested.

Okay, seriously. First exercise.

Let's think outside the box. Literally.

The box is yourself. Your perspective.

Let's think — not just from another person's perspective — but another *thing's* point of view.

I'll give you an example. I'm going to read a poem by H.W. Longfellow.

"Behold! a giant am I!
Aloft here in my tower,
With my granite jaws I devour
The maize, and the wheat, and the rye,
And grind them into flour."

No one answers.

"I look down over the farms;
In the fields of grain I see
The harvest that is to be,
And I fling to the air my arms,
For I know it is all for me."

I try to think of something. At first, I can't.
But then . . .

I do what she says.

The time goes by so fast. No chance to double-check myself or see if I messed up.

I just write.

I hear the scratches of everyone's pencils and pens. No other sound. It's kinda nice.

Is she serious?? My stomach lurches. Not again.

Mrs. Winn... okay to use the restroom first?

Why don't you read and *then* use the restroom?

She gives me this encouraging smile; I wonder if she understands my nervous stomach.

I take a deep, shuddery breath and try not to think about anyone judging my poem.

ahem

At the start, I'm stiff. And then slowly, I'm animated. Like a dance, my body moves in straight lines and squiggles...

...leaving behind every emotion. I say true things as I twist: things that are angry, happy, meaningful...

...petty, funny, weird, silly, or disgusting. I say it all in a strong, slender blur.

That's it.

clap clap clap clap clap

I smile, too.

I get up, but then change my mind and sit down. I realize I don't need to go anymore.

Also, I wanna hear the other poems.

Mrs. Winn calls on the others, one at a time. All the poems are pretty good. Daniel's is about a falling leaf. Leah's is about a blender. Sarah's is about a rickety chair.

And Juan's is flat-out clever.

about a bent-out-of-shape paper clip that was put back together but was never quite the same

haha = awww −

We do another exercise: Mrs. Winn has us write freestyle poems from the perspective of . . .

A brain-eating zombie!

We have fun with that. Juan even illustrates his poem.

And then . . .

That's all the time we have.

grooaan

I know we're meeting Thursday, but between now and *next* Monday, let's do a fun little project.

Every night, write one line of poetry. Then add a line each night until you have a whole poem by next week! We'll read them out loud.

We should do that at the next meeting, too.

I mean, everybody can write one line, then someone can add to that, and so on.

I really said that out loud?

We all leave. But I don't leave alone.

We had talked about that the other day, but nothing ever came out of it. I thought maybe she'd changed her mind.

We walk out of the building. My mom waits in her parked car, earbuds in. Probably listening to her new-agey playlist.

She looks at me eagerly—which is sooo annoying.
But also kinda . . . sweet.

I might as well have told her I won the lottery or a genie granted me three wishes.

So, uh, that girl, Leah, asked if I could go to her house to do homework.

I guess since you're already here, I can't, but —

oof!

A new friend?? Go, go!

She realizes what she's doing, midhug, and drops her arms.

Okay, I'm done.

With a grateful snort, I leave and go catch up with Leah.

Mia

I SLEPT OVER AT KEYA'S.

fretting about Trevor

HOUR 2:

blah blah blah Trevor

Z

yawn~

FOR SOME REASON, WE WENT TO BED EARLY THAT NIGHT.

RIGHT NOW, I'M UPDATING MY SNAPGAB PROFILE.

172

RUBY

We've met three times now.

poetry club

new desk configuration ("keeps it fresh" says Mrs. W.)

We even played my poetry game.

(It was a hit!)

giggle

haha

best line ↘

"The dentures struggled in the foamy water like a pink seahorse gasping for air."

Daniel dropped out, but a new boy and girl joined.

Not everyone shows up each time, but we've had a few regulars: me, Juan, and Leah. Speaking of Leah, I did go to her house last week. And I've gotta admit . . .

. . . it was weird.

But once we started talking about school, teachers, and poetry club, it became fun.

We had so much fun, we forgot to do homework. So I was up pretty late that night.

Turns out we have lots in common.

Also, there's stuff she does that I didn't even know I liked until I tried it with her. Like kitchen experiments.

hello, chocolate-mint-
beet smoothies!

=slorp=

She has lots of collections, too. So many, I couldn't help looking at all of them.

bowls of sea (actually, lake) glass

pages of stickers

jars of hotel soaps

my favorite:

tiny succulent plants

things I collect (not purposely):

dust bunnies

cat hairballs

pencil shavings

We've been hanging out at school ever since. It's so cool to have a new friend. The best part is she doesn't care about my bad social skills (probably 'cause of her shyness). Anyway, around her, that issue has sort of . . . disappeared.

Leah told me she and her sixth-grade friends drifted apart— just like Mia and me.

We both laugh.

183

Today, I've worked up the nerve to tell her about my stomach problems. Except for Mia, she's the only other kid I've ever shared that with.

I think for a minute.

We separate at the stairwell to go to our classes. As I wave bye, I see Mia at her locker down the hall.

Yeah, it's cool to have a new friend. And I can't help feeling kinda smug in front of someone who thinks I'm a loser.

But . . . I'm still a little sad.

'Cause even though Leah and I are getting tight doesn't mean I don't miss Mia. We used to laugh about stuff, too. We had a lot of inside jokes. We'd fight and make up. We just . . . got each other. And the weirdest thing about all that is . . .

. . . it wasn't that long ago.

Mia

WHAT JUST HAPPENED?

"Mia"?
Not "Meema"?

GABI AND KEYA ACT SO WEIRD WHENEVER I MENTION THE ELECTION.

SHOULDN'T THEY BE SUPPORTIVE? THEY SURE WERE AT FIRST.

NO.

Consorting with the enemy?!

I HEAD TO ENGLISH FEELING LIKE I'VE BEEN KICKED IN THE STOMACH.

SOMEHOW, I GET THROUGH ALL MY MORNING CLASSES. I GO TO MY LOCKER BEFORE LUNCH.

rubber bands

wipe

RUBY

Before we go, I'd like to remind you about the talent show coming up.

Poetry can be included!

In fact, I highly encourage it. What you did here today is a great example.

Everyone starts murmuring as we get up to leave.

I might do it. I love performing.

Uh. No kidding.

Not me. I'd die up there.

It's one thing to stand up in front of people you're pretty comfortable with, like at poetry club. I mean, that's where I feel most like myself now.

But it's another thing to get up in front of the whole school and be . . .

Still . . .

Nah.

198

But when I get home, I think about it (the talent show, not sloppy joes).

I don't think anyone's read a poem before.

So it'd be cool to try it.

I glance at the journal on my nightstand. It's not really a journal—more like a thick notebook that I got discounted and decorated with heart stickers. It's filled with two years of entries, stories, and poetry.

falling apart

keep out

Hi!

RUBY

stickers peeling off

"well loved," as our librarian, Ms. Regas, calls beat-up books

clawed by Buford

I grab it. Maybe there's something in here . . . ?

I'm the kind of person who, when I decide to do something, just does it. Mom says that runs in the family. That's good for some things, like homework and chores and stuff. But bad for other things . . .

. . . like deciding to recite a poem for the talent show.

But when I see it, I realize I have to. Well, not have to, but want to. Which is pretty much the same thing.

Because it's a poem that might help things.

Things that are broken.

Okay, it's a last-ditch effort, but why not? I'll just change the poem a little. So no one knows who it's about except me . . .

. . . and her.

Mia

TALENT SHOW! I'M SITTING WITH SOME GIRLS FROM THE SPIRIT SQUAD.

I WAS A MEMBER UNTIL I GOT TOO BUSY WITH SCHOOL AND STUDENT COUNCIL.

SO GLAD I STAYED FRIENDS WITH THEM.

203

BUT TREVOR IS REALLY WHY I DECIDED TO GO. DESPITE THE WEIRDNESS BETWEEN US, I'D PROMISED HIM.

Present time:

Hey, Mia.

Good luck next week.

Yeah. You too, Josh.

I liked your SnapGab page. You're really good at that stuff.

Thanks! I liked...

214

215

shrug

?

?

WELL... HE KNEW I DIDN'T WANNA GO UP THERE. THAT'S THE REASON HE DIDN'T PICK ME...

!

...ISN'T IT?

RUBY

Gulp.

I can't believe I'm doing this.

The place is packed. Am I the only nervous one?

Guess not.

I skipped rehearsal. I don't know why. I guess I was too scared, and it seemed like the right thing to do at the time. I kinda regret it now.

When Leah and Juan suggested doing the talent show, it was like they planted a bug in my ear. It buzzed around until I put a stop to it—by signing up.

I hope it was the right thing to do.

Brianna is still sweating. I hate to admit it but seeing that makes me feel better.

I want to tell him that all his talking is making me more nervous, but I don't. I'm trying to "use my filter," as adults say. It's hard, but I've gotten better.

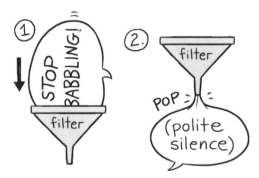

Now I wonder if he's babbling because **he's** nervous. Some people are like that.

Despite all the talking, he's nice. I wonder if we could be friends.

The bugs start eating my insides.

I'm both relieved and jealous that he goes on soon. Relieved 'cause I can check the audience's reaction to him. Jealous 'cause he's getting it over with.

He follows Mrs. D. A tiny sixth grader in huge platform shoes, holding a flute, follows, too.

In a few minutes, Mrs. D. goes onstage and welcomes everyone. Then she introduces the first act.

I laugh. Smart Girl is sassy.

When the flute player is done, there's a lot of clapping.

Thank you, Regina. Next up, we have a guitar solo from Juan Alvarez.

Guitar solo? I thought he was reciting a poem, like me. I can't help it. I slink over to the curtain to peek out.

BONK

I...

...um...

Whoa. I've never seen Juan nervous before. He's usually so confident.

He kinda gathers himself and stands straighter.

Okay. This is a song I made up.

He strums the guitar, playing a sad, soulful tune for a minute. He must be really comfortable playing; I think it helps him get over his nervousness. Soon—there's no other word for it—he starts to croon.*

The feather floats above so near, against the wind he sways.

I'd like to catch him in my palm, but out of reach he stays.

*my nana's word for what her favorite old-timey singers do

He stops singing but keeps playing the guitar. I wonder why Juan calls the feather "he." Then I remember Mrs. Winn teaching us about personification.

My mind drifts a little. Then the melody gets softer and softer until it ends.

Juan takes a bow and everyone claps. A few people whistle. I'm just shocked he didn't sing about a farting dog or something.

He waves and leaves, making a beeline to the snack table. I'm even more shocked.

He trusted me with that secret. Which means . . .

. . . we're friends, too?
Suddenly I forget to be nervous. That lasts about a second.

They follow Mrs. D. Dev looks kinda scared, and Brianna looks like she's seen ghost.

or swallowed one

I wait and listen backstage, feeling tense for them. After an unlucky start (ugh, mic feedback!), it sounds like they're doing okay. Before I know it, they're back.

Still looks like she's seen a ghost, but a friendly one

clap
clap
clap

I try not to be terrified, but then . . .

Okay! Trevor and Ruby, follow me!

Trevor rushes over, looking antsy, as though he wants to run a couple laps. He kinda jumps up and down, like he's warming up. I want to grab his shoulders and hold him in place.

Mrs. D. leads us to an area in between backstage and onstage. It's really dark and we're butted against tall curtains. She walks to the microphone and introduces Trevor, who practically runs onstage. Then Mrs. D. comes back and waits with me.

She must sense I'm nervous.

wonder
how
she
knows

It'll be okay. Just remember to breathe. If you got through rehearsal, you'll get through this!

I guess she forgot I wasn't there.

I hear the audience clap. Trevor rushes past me, looking pumped, sweaty, and holding a bunch of props. He fist-bumps some other kids backstage.

Mrs. D. gestures for me.
OMG. My turn.

OMGOMGOMG.

After waiting in the dark, it's so bright, I can't even see the audience. Which is good, I guess. That might make me turn and run. I hear some coughs, a few whispers, and one person in the middle of a sneezing fit.

I'm so glad I didn't tell anyone I was doing this.

I'm supposed to be "doing homework" at Leah's. My mom's so thrilled I have a new friend, she didn't bother to check in with Leah's parents.

I take a deep breath and try to remember Mrs. Winn's words:

Remember, for slam poetry, it's all about rhythm and passion.

Whether you're whispering, shouting, speeding up, or slowing down.

No matter how you feel, project confidence, and the confidence will follow.

I take a deep breath. I'm going all in. I've seen enough You-Tube videos to know I can't do it halfway.

I'd...uh...like to recite a poem.

This is for someone I really miss.

Here goes nothing.

IS SHE GOING TO SING?
OMG, PLEASE DON'T SING.

240

RUBY

They liked it!

I smile. Sort of. It's not something I'm used to doing much of. Usually, I feel like I'm trying too hard.

I give a little wave and head backstage. A few people rush over.

If I wasn't such a klutz, I'd be jumping for joy!

There are a bunch of acts left. I stick around and wait backstage. Juan sits next to me on the dusty floor and shares a bag of
honey-mustard pretzels.

Sorry. Uh. I'm trying to work on that... filter thing. I'm better on paper.

It's okay. Anyway, I don't know. We're both in manga. Sometimes I feel like he's looking at me.

I wish I had the guts to do, like, a grand gesture up there. Like a real love song or something.

You did do that. If he can't get a simple simile, then he's not worth it.

Hey, it wasn't *that* simple.

We laugh.

I wonder if I'll ever crush on somebody. I haven't yet. I may be tall for my age, but I still feel like I'm back in elementary school compared to a lot of seventh graders.

243

LIKES:

cartoons (or silly TV shows)

riding my bike →

DISLIKES:

smooch

romantic movies

"grown-up" food like asparagus and lentils

smooch

sappy couples

Well, except for writing. Mrs. Winn tells me my writing style is:

mature

After the show, we all head out. I wave bye to Juan. I live only a block away, so I start to walk home.

Hey, Ruby! Wait up.

What the heck? What does she want?

I loved your poem. I never, like, saw that side of you.

Uh... thanks.

Where's Mia?

She, um...

I think she left.

Her voice trails off.

Sorry, I was sitting with my parents, so I don't really know what happened.

Oh.

We've barely talked in, like, ages.

I'm sorry, Ruby.

245

There's kind of an uncomfortable silence.

Not to change the subject, but...

...I'm thinking of joining the poetry club.

Really?

Yeah. Your act kinda... inspired me. Anyway, swim season is almost over, and... well, I really like poetry.

I remember Dev saying that. If I had been brave enough to ask her to join that day in the cafeteria, she might already be a member. But there was no way I was gonna approach her with Mia there (and all their friends).

Okay. Next meeting is Monday after school. Room 216.

I know. I took a flyer.

She waves and heads back to the school.

I continue walking home, kinda sad and confused. Now I don't know if reciting that poem was worth it or not. I mean, on one hand it was, 'cause it proved that I'm good at slam poetry! It also got Keya to join the club.

But the main reason I did it was to try to . . . well . . . reach out and make things right, I guess. And that didn't work.

In fact . . .

. . . I think it made everything worse.

I HAD PROMISED TREVOR WE'D MEET AFTER THE SHOW AND GO TO TAYSTEE'S.

(back before things got weirder between us than Taystee's last Flavor of the Month)

mushroom chip

I'M SURPRISED HE STILL *WANTED* TO MEET.

im so so so srry. somthg happnd

what

DO I REALLY WANT TO GET INTO IT? IT'S TOO MORTIFYING.

RUBY

It all began when Mia started middle school.

pre-braces

1st DAY of
6th GRADE

I was in fifth grade—even though I looked about three grades older. (I'm really a year and a half younger, if you wanna get technical.) We were inseparable.

four inches taller

signature look →

ladybug necklace that got stolen the first week of school

She was a little nerdy but outgoing. And back then, she wasn't wound so tightly. Soon, she started making new friends and trying every activity known to humankind.

Competitive pizza-eating-ribbon-tying-gymnastics

She stuck it out with student council. She made "Citizenship Czar"* in seventh grade. Then she was elected treasurer for eighth.

IT MAKES ¢ENT$

to vote 4 MIA

the pun stuff started young

The hard part: her new friends were (way) more exciting, smarter, and popular than me.

*since changed to "Citizenship Champ" after Benji Sokolov's family complained

And they weren't . . . well, misfits.

(may be exaggerating slightly)

Not that Mia ever said anything about that. Not to my face, anyway. But I knew I was holding her back. Especially once I got to middle school.

At first, she didn't totally ignore me or anything. We still hung out after school.

← Phineas and Ferb

But I knew she was starting to get uncomfortable. And embarrassed. I didn't fit in with her idea of "popular" and "perfect."

popular perfect

hey

She started to keep her distance at school and pretend she didn't see me. Stuff like that. Later, if we were in public together, she'd make up these rules about what "we" should or shouldn't say.

The more uncomfortable she got, the madder I got.

Eventually, I started taking the hint and stopped hanging around her.

But somehow, even now, I don't wanna let go. Even though I do things to upset her. And even though she can seem so self-absorbed and shallow.

Maybe 'cause I know who she still is underneath. I know her

biggest secrets. I know that she kissed Rahul Patel in fourth grade (after he ate pepperoni pizza, yuck). I know that she once wore shredded jeans to camp and the director made her cover the holes with duct tape. I know she secretly did Minecraft until seventh grade. I know she once tried a cheap self-tanner, and when it turned her orange, she faked a cold and stayed home till it faded.

I know how she loves dried mangos, and old *Phineas and Ferb* cartoons, and holding her breath in the pool as long as she can (I had to call for the lifeguard once!), and old songs, and thrift stores, and Taystee's weirdest flavors (jalapeño, really?).

Maybe that's why I don't wanna let go.
Maybe that's why I did what I did at the talent show.

But . . . I'm finally realizing that even a personal poem I wrote
and performed in front of everyone won't sway her.

That was my last-ditch effort.

It's really over.

A LITTLE OVER A WEEK TILL THE ELECTION. NEED TO SHOVE ASIDE ALL PERSONAL PROBLEMS UNTIL IT'S OVER.

BUT THIS MORNING, I GOT A TEXT FROM KEYA.

262

SHE LEADS ME TO A FITTING ROOM IN BACK AND WE SIT ON THE BENCH.

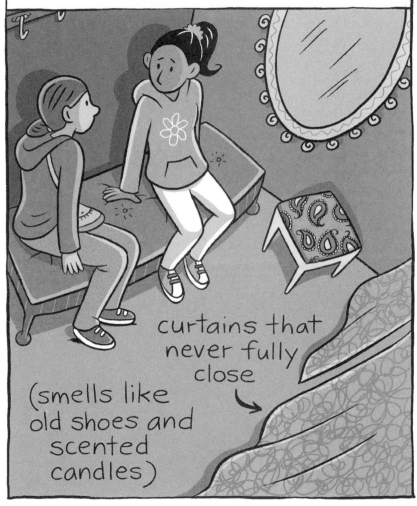

curtains that never fully close

(smells like old shoes and scented candles)

WITHOUT MEANING TO, HER VOICE RISES.

happens when she's...

☑ excited
☑ angry
☑ happy
☑ passionate
☑ all of the above
(we go deaf)

Well, it's not like you guys have time to listen.

I STORM OUT.

You're too busy being your own bffs. Swimming, band, after-swimming and band...

RUBY

Monday. Poetry club.

273

WINN WORD
OF THE WEEK:
"valorous"

There it is.

Proof that Mia is mad at me. More than "silent treatment" mad. She hates me.

HATE METER:

silent treatment

barely tolerates

wants me banished to a desert island— surrounded by jellyfish and sharks

I try to get her out of my mind. I go back to listening to Keya. Since it's her first meeting, I don't know how good she is at writing poetry, but she sure loves reading it. And listening to ours. She laughed at a funny rap Juan and I made up about smelly armpits. Mrs. Winn laughed, too, even though she looked like she wanted to throw up.

glurgh

This month of poetry club has been, like, the best month of my middle school life. I can't believe I didn't want to do it at first. It seems like a thousand years since I felt like I belonged anywhere.

But now Mia is making me feel bad about it.

Not only is she mad about the talent show, but it's obvious she's mad that Keya joined poetry. As if I stole her friend.

Well, she can be that way. But I'm not giving up any friends. She's gonna have to share.

We'll see how that goes.

THAT'S HOW I FEEL RIGHT NOW WATCHING JOSH.

FOR A MONTH, I'VE DEVOTED EVERYTHING TO THIS CAMPAIGN.

flyers! VOTE for MIA!

posters! MIA!!

buttons! MIA

intercom announcements! MIA!

social media! Vote 4 Mia!

AND WHAT'S HE DOING? CHATTING UP THE GIRLS!

doesn't help that he's cute and charming

charisma glow

I JUST HAVE TO BELIEVE THAT ALL THIS HARD WORK WILL PAY OFF. IT'S *GOTTA*.

ESPECIALLY SINCE THIS IS COSTING ME MY FRIENDS AND BF.

THERE'S AN AWKWARD SILENCE. SO TIRED OF IT.

Hey. So...you mad at me?

Not mad... just frustrated, I guess.

WE WALK OVER TO A QUIET HALLWAY.

It's just, like, been hard to talk to you. You keep these secrets, and—

281

282

THAT SETS ME OFF. THIS ELECTION IS SHOWING ME EVERYONE *ELSE'S* TRUE COLORS.

Unsupportive Orange

Impatient Indigo

Critical Crimson

Fine. We'll take a break.

A **LONG** break.

Mia—

CAN THIS DAY GET ANY WORSE?

DON'T ANSWER THAT.

RUBY

Mrs. Langer stares at us without blinking. I start to wonder if she has eyelids.

I look at Mia and she looks at me.

grunt

sigh

Well, unfortunately, fighting in school automatically means detention.

I groan. I got detention once, in sixth grade, after accidentally knocking down a hall monitor on my way to the restroom. (The hall monitor was drinking hot tea, so . . .) I've been trying to avoid it ever since. There goes my record.

It's been [0] days since my last detention.

Mom is channeling all her nervous energy into bouncing her crossed leg. Augh, make it stop!

Mia and I both look hopeful.

Mrs. Langer looks down at her desktop, thinking. Her desk is covered with framed photos. She must have a huge family. Sometimes I forget that teachers have actual lives. I think Mrs. Langer is in her sixties, so she probably has grandkids.

We nod.

I didn't know that. Is there anything Mrs. Winn **doesn't** do?

I don't say it out loud: that working together means we might kill each other.

But between detention and that . . .

Okay.

We all look at Mia.

Um, is there any way we could do this *after* the election?

Actually, Mia, I think this would be good for you.

Now.

Okay.

Everyone looks relieved.

It's settled. I'll talk to Mrs. Winn.

We get up and leave, the grown-ups chatting softly (as if we can't hear) while Mia and I trail behind, not talking to each other.

...so unlike them. Even if they've been feuding....

Pretty typical....

Suddenly . . .

Not another stomach attack!

Stupid Mia.
It's all her fault.

Mia

298

RUBY

Here's what happened yesterday after dinner:

We had to come up with two poetry projects for Mrs. Winn's
after-school program. Which we didn't want to do . . .
   . . . together.

But we did. At first, it was weird.

And awkward.

And kinda infuriating.

But then Mom walked in.

You know I hate to interfere...

I actually choked on a chip.

So we checked it out. Or Mia checked it out while I hung back at first. After a minute, I quietly tiptoed over, as if walking normally would make her explode or something. She didn't say anything, so I peeked over a shoulder.

I was ready for her to tell me off. But instead, she looked closer.

She didn't say anything for a couple seconds. Then:

She was quiet for another moment. But not mad-quiet. Just thinking.

She told me her idea. I had to admit, it was pretty good. We talked about it without arguing. And then we scrolled more.

And we did.

Somehow, we managed to spend two hours together, doing things, without ticking each other off. It almost seemed like old times.

And today . . .

We get them started by passing out magazine pages, and their excitement grows. Sometimes I even catch myself smiling over something cute that a kid says. I notice two strange things:

1. I don't have that usual left-out feeling I have at school. These kids are easy to talk to. And their enthusiasm is catching.

2. I start to forget why I'm here in the first place.

Oh yeah.

While the students work, Mia comes over.

Your poem was... really good, Ruby.

Yeah? Thanks.

You weren't even nervous reading it.

I used to get really nervous. But now I'm used to it.

I'm getting nervous about my speech on Monday. I haven't even finished writing it.

nod

It's been a long time since she's confessed anything to me. I can't believe I say this:

A small boy in glasses tugs on my shirt.

After I help him, we move on to the next project. Mia and I pass out paint chips—the kind that have five different gradating colors and artsy names.

Your job is to connect each word with other words.

You can use sentences or even just a single word. Put together, it'll form a cool poem.

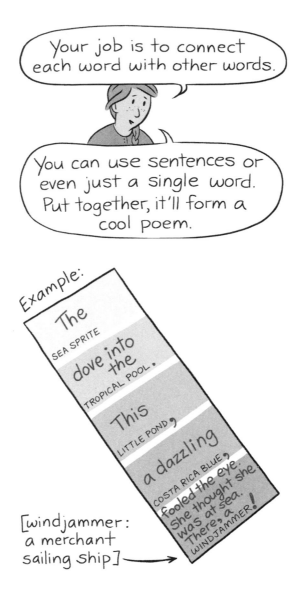

Example:

The
SEA SPRITE
dove into the
TROPICAL POOL.
This
LITTLE POND,
a dazzling
COSTA RICA BLUE,
fooled the eye.
She thought she was at sea.
There, a
WINDJAMMER!

[windjammer: a merchant sailing ship] ——→

At first, there's arguing over who gets what colors. Luckily, Mia and I thought ahead and got duplicates.

As the kids work, Mrs. Winn walks over.

As if on cue, a fourth grader named Lydia calls out.

Miss Ruby or Miss Mia? Can you help me?

Mia goes to her while I check on some other kids. What I love is, they don't look at me like I don't belong. They look at me with . . .

. . . well, respect.

The same way I look at Mrs. Winn.

It's then and there that I start thinking, maybe, just maybe . . .

. . . I might want to be a teacher, too.

WOW.

OKAY, NOW I *AM* THINKING OF THE ELECTION. BUT NOT IN THE USUAL WAY.

I didn't treat Ruby fairly. What about everyone else?

Keya? Gabi?

Even... Josh?

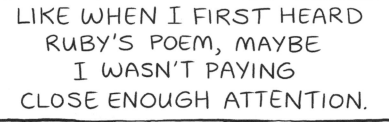

LIKE WHEN I FIRST HEARD
RUBY'S POEM, MAYBE
I WASN'T PAYING
CLOSE ENOUGH ATTENTION.

I've gotta go.
Thanks, Gabs.
And sorry for...
you know,
everything.

smooch

Me too.
Bye, Meema.

RUBY

I'm writing in my journal when I get the text.

Whoa.

I stare at the screen for a long time.

Do I?

Is she finally forgiving me for everything?

Am I forgiving **her**?

Typical Mia, making peace by asking for a favor.

Still, she **is** reaching out.

Soon, I'm in her room. Hard to believe.

We don't get started right away. We talk. For a long time. I guess we need to "hash things out," as grown-ups say. Now I know where that expression comes from.

hash-like convo:
bits and pieces
of everything

I've gotta admit,
I didn't really... well,
listen-listen to your
poem at the talent show.

But after yesterday...
I went back and
watched the video.

She did?

It was really,
really good.

Thanks.

She looks at me and I half smile. She laughs a little.

An' I'm working on that. But I get jealous that you're so smart and have it all together.

So I tell myself you're stuck-up and self-absorbed.

That makes *me* a jerk.

Mia thinks about this.

You're not a jerk. And I'm not "together."

Also, I get jealous, too.

Say what?

You're sooo good at writing. And poetry. Sometimes I feel like there's nothing special I do.

A pause.

332

I help her. When we're done, she reads it aloud to me.

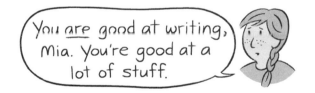

This reminds me of when we used to write stories together. Remember that one we made up three years ago?

THE (by Ruby AND Mia) ADVENTURES of RUBMIA

← got about 1/3 through

← the kind of nickname Trevor and I avoid

You _are_ good at writing, Mia. You're good at a lot of stuff.

Thanks.

I do miss Mrs. Winn's class.

She goes silent for a few seconds, remembering, probably. Then she looks up and smiles.

Mia

First...

But it's okay. I'll stick with student council and focus on that. Because I still want to make Lakefront the most awesome place for students. And I think that's the best way for me to do it.

I PAUSE AND TAKE ANOTHER DEEP BREATH.

Also, I'd like to thank a few people for their help.

Gabi Mills, Keya Devar, and Trevor Enders. You put up with me when I was a campaign-zilla. Thank you for everything!

RUBY

Writing in my journal. Got a lot to say lately.

Good things this time. Well, mostly. Some iffy, too. Like Joe Lungo, who thinks spitballs are the best way to get the teacher's attention, even when I'm in the line of fire.

Also, asparagus, which is what Mom served on top of a perfectly good pile of spaghetti tonight. What gives?

Speaking of food (and pee), I went back to the doctor to get my nervous stomach checked. This time, the doctor sent me to my very first . . .

She gave me a mental "tool kit" of tricks to start helping me with anxiety. Like meditating, breathing, and my favorite . . .

I had only one session, but I guess I'm meeting again with her in a few weeks. She seemed okay. Well, more than okay. She seemed to get me.

I text Juan and invite him to Taystee's. He texts back, telling me he wrote a poem about Taystee's. I believe it. Juan can make a poem about anything.

Once wrote one about a bug he found in his braces

My phone dings again. I'm still not used to it. I'm used to the quiet.

Half an hour later:

EPILOGUE: *Mia*

356

361

I, uh, even wrote you a poem.

A...a poem?

Yep. Me. I wrote one.

I'M "TOUCHED," AS MY MOM SAYS WHENEVER SOMEONE BUYS ONE OF HER FIGURINES ON ETSY. AS FAR AS I KNOW, TREVOR'S NEVER WRITTEN A POEM OUTSIDE ENGLISH CLASS.

ahem